Usborne First Experiences

Going to the dentist

Anne Civardi
Illustrated by Stephen Cartwright

Reading Consultant: Betty Root

There is a little yellow duck hiding on every two pages. Can you find it?

The Judds

This is the Judd family. Jake is six and Jessie is three.
Jake has a toothache so Dad calls the dentist.

Off to the dentist

After lunch Mom takes Jake to see Dr. Drake, the dentist. He is going to check Jessie's teeth as well.

In the waiting room

Jake and Jessie play in the waiting room until it is their turn to see Dr. Drake. Jaspar, the dog, plays too.

The dental assistant

Miss Day, the dental assistant, helps Dr. Drake. She takes
Jake and Jessie in to see him. Jaspar stays behind.

Dr. Drake, the dentist

The dentist sees Jake and Jessie in his office. He says
Mom can come in and watch.

Jessie's turn

Jessie is first. She sits in a special chair that can go up and down and back and forth.

Checking Jessie's teeth

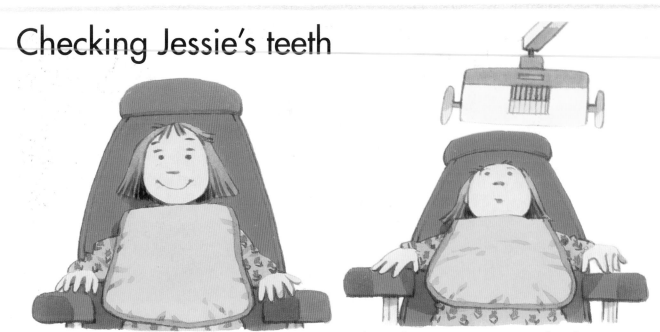

Jessie wears a bib round her neck. There is a spotlight above her which shines into her mouth.

Dr. Drake wears a mask over his mouth and nose and rubber gloves on his hands.

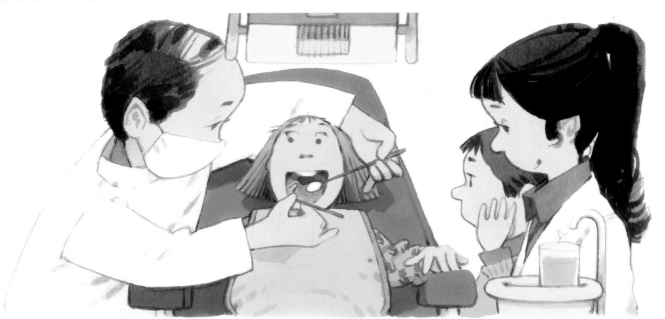

He uses a little mirror so that he can see all over her teeth and an instrument called a probe.

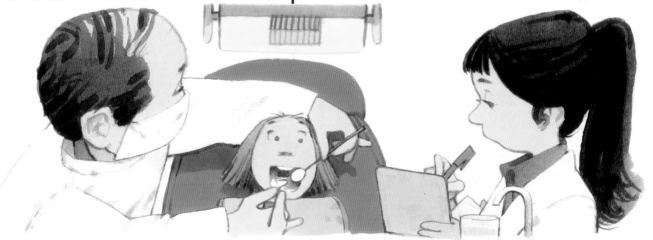

Dr. Drake looks at each of Jessie's teeth. Miss Day writes down notes about them.

Jessie is finished

The dentist is very pleased with Jessie. She has no holes in her teeth. Now she can rinse out her mouth.

Jake's turn

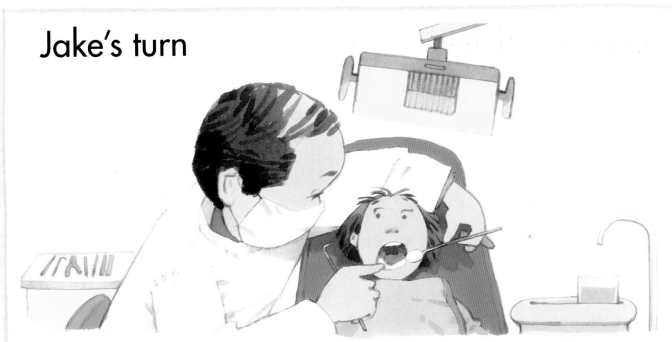

But when he checks Jake's teeth he finds a small hole in the one that aches.

Before he fills the hole, he gives Jake an injection into his gum to make it go numb. It hurts just a little.

Jake has a filling

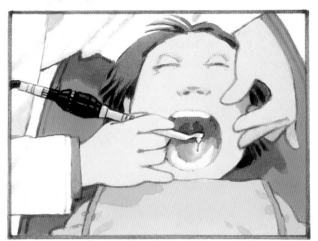

Dr. Drake drills away the bad bit of the tooth. Miss Day keeps it dry with a special instrument.

Then she mixes the filling to put into the hole. It looks just like silver.

JAKE'S FILLED TOOTH

THIS IS WHAT JAKE'S FILLED TOOTH LOOKS LIKE NOW

Dr. Drake presses the filling mixture into the clean hole. Now Jake will not have a toothache anymore.

Looking after your teeth

UNHEALTHY TEETH AND GUMS LOOK LIKE THIS

HEALTHY TEETH AND GUMS LOOK LIKE THIS

Before they go home, Dr. Drake shows Jake and Jessie what will happen if they do not clean their teeth.

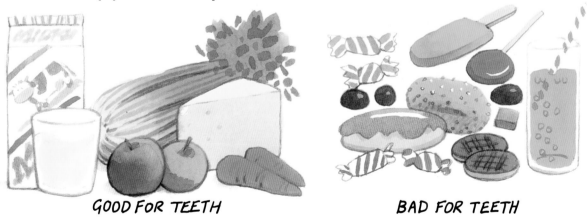

GOOD FOR TEETH

BAD FOR TEETH

He says that fruits, vegetables, cheese and milk are good for teeth. But sweet, sticky things are not.

Miss Day shows them how to clean their teeth really well. This gets rid of old food which can cause holes.

Jake and Jessie must clean their front and back teeth all over every day to keep them clean and healthy.

Making an appointment

On their way out, Jake and Jessie make an appointment to see the dentist in six months' time.

First published in 1986. This enlarged edition first published in 1992. Usborne Publishing Ltd, 83-85 Saffron Hill, London EC1N 8RT, England. © Usborne Publishing Ltd, 1992.